YEARLING BOOKS/YOUNG YEARLINGS/YEARLING CLASSICS are designed especially to entertain and enlighten young people. Patricia Reilly Giff, consultant to this series, received her bachelor's degree from Marymount College and a master's degree in history from St. John's University. She holds a Professional Diploma in Reading and a Doctorate of Humane Letters from Hofstra University. She was a teacher and reading consultant for many years, and is the author of numerous books for young readers.

For a complete listing of all Yearling titles,
write to Dell Readers Service,
P.O. Box 1045,
South Holland, IL 60473.

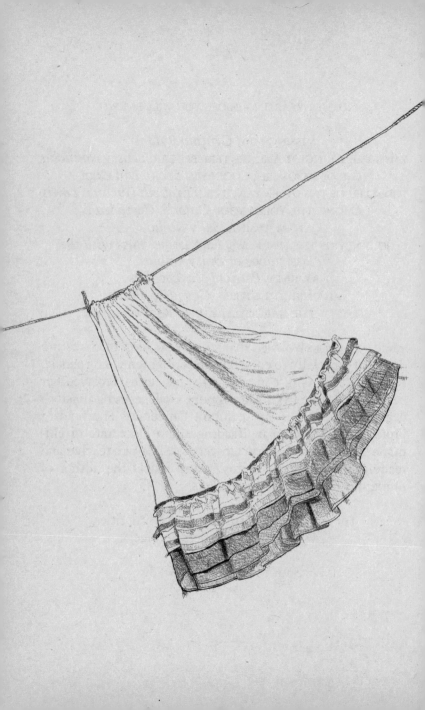

GARY SOTO

THE SKIRT

Illustrated by Eric Velasquez

A YEARLING BOOK

Published by
Dell Publishing
a division of
Bantam Doubleday Dell Publishing Group, Inc.
1540 Broadway
New York, New York 10036

ISBN: 0-440-40924-1

Reprinted by arrangement with Delacorte Press

Printed in the United States of America

May 1994

10 9 8 7 6

CWO

The SKIRT

Chapter **1**

After stepping off the bus, Miata Ramirez turned around and gasped, "Ay!" The school bus lurched, coughed a puff of stinky exhaust, and made a wide turn at the corner. The driver strained as he worked the steering wheel like the horns of a bull.

Miata yelled for the driver to stop. She

started running after the bus. Her hair whipped against her shoulders. A large book bag tugged at her arm with each running step, and bead earrings jingled as they banged against her neck.

"My skirt!" she cried loudly. "Stop!"

She had forgotten her *folklórico* skirt. It was still on the bus. She and her best friend, Ana, both fourth graders, had been bothered by boys. The two girls moved from seat to seat. The boys followed and taunted them with a rubber frog. Giggling, the girls moved away from Larry and Juan. They especially moved far away from Rodolfo, a boy with green eyes and hair so shiny black that it was nearly blue. He was trying to write his name on their arms and asked them to play basketball with him after school.

"Come on," he had argued. "It's Friday. There is no school tomorrow."

But Miata and Ana had ignored him as they moved from seat to seat. They looked out the window and nibbled secretly on animal crackers when the boys weren't bothering them.

"Please stop!" Miata yelled as she ran after the bus. Her legs kicked high and her lungs burned from exhaustion.

She needed that skirt. On Sunday after church she was going to dance *folklórico*. Her troupe had practiced for three months. If she was the only girl without a costume, her parents would wear sunglasses out of embarrassment. Miata didn't want that.

The skirt had belonged to her mother when she was a child in Hermosillo, Mexico. What is Mom going to think? Miata asked herself. Her mother was always scolding Miata for losing things. She lost combs, sweaters, books, lunch money, and homework. One time she even lost her shoes at school. She had left them on the baseball field where she had raced against two boys. When she returned to get them, the shoes were gone.

Worse, she had taken her skirt to school to show off. She wanted her friends to see it. The skirt was old, but a rainbow of shiny ribbons still made it pretty. She put it on during lunchtime and danced for some of her friends. Even a teacher stopped to watch.

What am I going to do now? Miata asked herself. She slowed to a walk. Her hair had come undone. She felt hot and sticky.

She could hear the bus stopping around the corner. Miata thought of running through a neighbor's yard. But that would only get her in trouble.

"Oh, man," Miata said under her breath. She felt like throwing herself on the ground and crying. But she knew that would only make things worse. Her mother would ask, "Why do you get so dirty all the time?"

Miata turned the corner and saw a paper plane sail from the rear window. It hung in the air for a second and then crashed into a ragged rosebush as the bus drove off. She carefully plucked the plane from the bush. When she unfolded it she discovered Rodolfo's math quiz. He had a perfect score. A gold star glittered under his name.

"He's smart," she said. "For a boy."

She crumpled the paper plane and looked up. The bus was now out of sight. So was her beautiful skirt.

"Darn it," Miata muttered. Shrugging her book bag over her shoulder, she started walking home. Miata wanted to blame the boys but knew it was her fault. She should have told the boys to leave Ana and her alone. She should have snatched that frog and thrown it out the window.

What am I going to do now? she asked herself. She prayed that Ana would find the skirt on the bus. She's got to see it, Miata thought. *It's right there. Just look, Ana.*

As Miata rounded the corner onto her block she saw her brother, Little Joe, and his friend Alex. They were walking with cans smashed onto the heels of their shoes, laughing and pushing each other. Their mouths were fat with gum.

Little Joe waved a dirty hand at Miata. Miata waved back and tried to smile.

"Start us?" Joe asked. "We're going to have a race."

Miata stopped and said, "Okay, but make it fast."

Little Joe and Alex lined up. Bodies leaning, they were ready to race. She counted, *uno . . . dos . . .* , and on *tres* they were off. Miata pressed her hands to her ears. The racket of the cans was deafening.

Her brother was the first to touch the tree.

"I won," Little Joe said.

But Alex argued because one of Little Joe's cans had come off his shoe. "You cheated," Alex yelled.

"No, I didn't," Little Joe yelled back. His hands were doubled into fists.

Miata left them arguing. She climbed the steps to her house. She was troubled. If Ana doesn't pick up the skirt, she thought, I'll have to dance in a regular skirt.

It was Friday, late afternoon. It looked like a long weekend of worry.

Chapter 2

Miata's family had moved from Los Angeles. Their new home was in Sanger, a small town in the San Joaquin Valley. Her father had gotten tired of the bad air and the long commute to his job at an auto-parts store. One day when he returned home, he called his wife and children to the kitchen table. He asked what they thought about moving to a different place.

At first Miata didn't like the idea of moving. But now she was living in a house, not an apartment. Now she was in the dance club at school. Now she had a best friend, Ana. The move had been good for Miata.

Her mother, Alicia, came into the living room just as Miata was throwing her book bag onto the floor. The book bag landed with a crash.

"*¡Ay, Dios!*" her mother chirped. "You scared me, *prieta*. I didn't hear you come in."

Her mother was holding an old cloth diaper. It was now her cleaning rag. She was wearing jeans and a work shirt splotched with old paint. She had been cleaning the house. The piles of newspapers were thrown out, the magazines were neatly stacked, and the air smelled fresh as a lemon. The crocheted afghan on the couch was straight. The water in the aquarium was clear, not green. Her father's ashtray had been emptied and wiped clean.

Miata decided to tell her mother about the skirt later. She gave her mother a hug and went to her bedroom. She sat on her bed, counting the minutes until Ana would arrive. She looked down at her wristwatch. It was three thirty-five.

Ana's getting off the bus right now, she told herself. And I bet she has my skirt.

In her mind, Miata could see Ana. Little Ana had curly hair and a galaxy of freckles on her face. Miata had known one other Mexican girl who had freckles. But that girl lived in Los Angeles, and she wasn't as nice as Ana.

Miata did her math homework, which took only ten minutes because math was her best subject, but still the telephone didn't ring. Miata grew so impatient she counted to one hundred, backward and forward.

Miata scooted off the bed and went to the hallway, where the telephone sat on a small table. She picked up the telephone; a long buzz rang in her ear.

Miata hung up and returned to her bedroom, where she changed into her play clothes. She figured that by the time she had finished changing, the telephone would ring. It would be Ana calling.

"Come on, Ana, just call," she whined.

The last button on her shirt was buttoned. She was completely dressed. Miata took off her earrings and wristwatch. She straightened her horse-print bedspread. She put away the clothes that were on the floor. She even sorted her crayons. But the telephone still didn't ring.

"Please call, Ana," she whispered. She sat down on her bed and started poking at a sliver in her little finger. The sliver was from the bench where they ate lunch. It had been bothering her all day.

Miata decided to call Ana. She tiptoed to the hallway. She dialed Ana's house and heard, *"Bueno."*

In Spanish, Miata asked if Ana was home from school.

"Todavía no está aquí," the voice said. Miata figured that it was Ana's grandmother. Miata asked if Ana would call her when she got home. The grandmother said that she would.

Miata went to the kitchen. Her mother was peeling potatoes. The radio was turned to the Mexican station.

"How was school?" her mother asked. "Here, you finish this." She handed the half-skinned potato and the potato peeler to Miata. Miata started working, the skin of potatoes flying into the sink.

"School was okay," Miata answered. "I got an *A* on my spelling test. Mrs. Garcia says that I have a good memory." Just as she said this she remembered her skirt. If my memory is so great, she thought, why did I forget my skirt on the bus?

"Are you ready for the dance this weekend?" Miata's mother asked. "Ana's mother called and said you two should practice Sunday morning before church. But I told her we didn't have time."

Miata didn't say anything. She worked faster, the peels flying like rubber bands.

"Your father will be so proud," her mother said. She opened the refrigerator and took out a piece of meat.

Miata was peeling her third potato when the telephone rang. She dropped the potato and potato peeler and screamed, "I got it."

She raced through the living room to the hallway. On the fourth ring she answered the telephone. "Ana?" Miata asked, her heart pounding.

"Yeah?"

"Did you find it?"

"Find what?" Ana's voice was confused.

"My skirt! It was on the bus. Didn't you see it?" Miata's voice was desperate.

"Your skirt?"

"I left my skirt on the bus. Didn't you see it?"

"No. You mean you lost your *folklórico* skirt?"

Miata could hear sounds in the kitchen. The steak was sizzling in a frying pan. Water was running from the faucet. She could hear her father. He was home from work and laughing about something. But would he be in a good mood when she told him that she had lost her skirt?

"Come over tomorrow morning," Miata told Ana. "You have to help me out." She hung up and returned to the kitchen to peel potatoes.

Chapter 3

At dinner, they had steak, *frijoles*, and *papas fritas*. They also had a small salad that was mostly lettuce. This was her father's favorite meal. Everyone in the family, even Little Joe, called it *carne del viernes*. This was their father's reward for a week of hard work: a large meal and then a baseball game on television.

Miata's father, José, now worked as a welder. He worked mostly on tractors and trailers. The money was good, nearly as good as his pay in Los Angeles.

Her mother stabbed a tomato slice hiding behind a sheet of lettuce. She nudged Miata. "Tell *Papi* about your spelling."

"I got an *A*," she said, smiling. "Next week I could be spelling bee champion if Dolores doesn't beat me." Dolores was a small girl with a big brain.

"*Qué bueno,*" her father said as he cut a *papa* with his fork. Steam rose from the parted *papa*. "Spelling is important," he said between bites. "One day you will get a good job if you know lots of words."

"You could be a doctor," her mother said.

"*Mi'ja*, you could fix me up," her father said. He rotated his aching arm. Her father was always getting injured. Today a pipe had fallen from the truck and struck his arm. A purplish bruise had already appeared.

"Did you hurt yourself?" her mother asked. She put down her fork. Her face was dark with worry.

"Does it hurt?" Little Joe asked.

"Only when I do this," José said. He stood up and punched Little Joe on the arm, softly.

Little Joe laughed and told his father, "That doesn't hurt."

The conversation turned to sports. Although they were living in the valley, José could pick up the Los Angeles Dodgers on television. It was a beautiful May. His Dodgers were two up on the San Francisco Giants. This made him happy. Last year the Giants had beaten them.

"Next year, Little Joe," he said to his

son, "you'll be eight and you can start playing ball."

Little Joe looked at his father but didn't answer. His cheeks were stuffed with tortilla.

Miata's father finished his meal. He patted his stomach and went to the living room with a glass of iced tea. Miata helped her mother in the kitchen.

"That was great, Mom," Miata said. She scraped the plates and put them in the sink.

"Thank you," her mother said. Her mother was happy as a singing canary. She turned on the radio. "I'm going to be so proud on Sunday."

"What's happening Sunday?" Little Joe asked. A milk mustache gleamed on his lip.

"Miata's dancing," her mother said.

Miata swallowed hard. She thought of

her skirt. Will I be able to get it by Sunday? she wondered.

While they were drying the dishes they heard a loud sigh from the living room. Miata looked at her mother. Her mother looked at her and asked, *"¿Qué pasó?"* Miata shrugged her shoulders.

"The game is rained out," her father groaned over the sound of the television. "How could it rain in San Diego? And on a Friday."

Disappointed, her father came into the kitchen with his empty glass. He rinsed it out and placed it on the drainboard. He told Miata, "Let's go get some ice cream, then."

Miata nearly jumped into her father's arms. She dried her hands on a dish towel and pulled her father to the front door. She hoped he would buy cookies and cream, her favorite.

They got into his truck. It was a '68 Chevy with windows that rattled. The old truck could get up to sixty miles per hour. Three red wires dangled from the broken radio. The speedometer was broken. Its needle leaped like a flea now and then, but it always fell back.

The Ramirez family was new in town, but made friends easily. A woman watering her flower bed waved at the passing truck. Miata waved back with both of her hands.

"It's nice here," her father said as he looked around the neighborhood. "The air is clean as a whistle." He turned on the broken radio and began to whistle a song.

Since moving to Sanger, Miata's father seemed happier. He had gotten tired of Los Angeles. He had grown up on a farm in Mexico. City life was not for him.

At the gas station a friend from work

waved. Her father stopped whistling. He waved, tooted his horn twice, and yelled, "The game's rained out."

"But the Giants are on channel twenty-four," the man yelled. He was inflating an inner tube.

"Los Gigantes," her father sneered, and shook his head. He was a loyal Dodgers fan, through and through.

They passed the school. Miata was reminded of her *folklórico* skirt. She had been talking loudly over the roar of the engine, telling her father about Little Joe and the cans on his shoes. But she stopped her chatter and bit her lip. She stared silently at the fenced parking lot. The buses were kept there. They passed the buses and Miata got on her knees. She looked back at them.

It's in one of them, she thought. Me and Ana have to get it tomorrow.

At the store her father bought a carton of Neapolitan ice cream. It was strawberry, chocolate, and vanilla. All three different flavors would dance on her tongue when they got back home.

Chapter 4

It was Saturday morning. Miata and Ana were sitting on the front steps of the library. The day was clear and beautiful. A single white cloud cut across the sky. A bird hopped on the lawn.

"Just tell your mom," Ana said. "She won't get mad."

"I can't," Miata said. She wagged her

head, and her hair swished against her shoulders. "She's always telling me that I lose things."

"But it's true."

Miata looked at Ana in a funny way. "Whose side are you on?"

Ana smiled and answered, "Yours, of course."

But Ana was thinking of her own things that Miata had lost. She had lost two erasers, some marbles, a rubber ball, a favorite pretty feather, the glittery magic wand from her Tío Benny, a magnifying glass from a cereal box—things now lost in the wide, wide world.

"Good. Because you're going to help me get my skirt back."

"Me?" asked Ana, her shoulders hunched slightly. "What am I supposed to do?"

"Just do what I do," Miata told her.

They went inside the library. The canary behind the desk was beating its tiny beak against a silver bell. The noise didn't seem to bother anyone.

Neither did the constant hum of the drinking fountain. The two of them stepped on the fountain's pedal. The water sprang up, nearly hitting Miata in the face.

"Watch it," Miata screamed, jumping back.

The librarian looked in their direction. She raised a finger to her pursed mouth. It meant to be quiet.

The girls stopped at a world globe. They spun it. For a few seconds they were dizzy as they saw Africa, Europe, and the Americas spin before their eyes.

"My father and mother are from here," Miata said, tapping northern Mexico. "From Sonora."

"My parents were born in L.A. But my

grandfather is from here," Ana said, tapping the state of Guerrero. "We went there once. I thought it was going to be hot, but it wasn't."

They gave the globe a spin and left the children's corner. They ventured into the reference room. A man wearing large earphones was listening to English tapes. He was an old man with leathery skin, a *Mexicano*. The man was quietly saying the words "dust, rocks, suitcase."

Miata and Ana checked out four books each and left the library. Instead of heading home, they walked in the direction of the school parking lot.

Miata was getting scared, and Ana was already scared. They felt like thieves.

"It's like stealing," Ana said.

"No, it's not," Miata countered. "It's my skirt."

"What if someone sees us?"

"Who?"

They stopped in their tracks when they saw Rodolfo, the boy with green eyes. They pressed themselves against a tree as Rodolfo rode by on his bike. His knees were grass-stained. His hair was tousled.

"He almost saw us," Ana whispered.

"He's nothing but a big bother," Miata said. For a second she recalled his perfect score in math. Next time she was stuck on a problem she would seek him out.

They watched him jump a curb. He pushed his hand into his pocket for a fistful of sunflower seeds. When he turned the corner Miata and Ana came out from behind the tree.

"That was close." Miata sighed. "Let's go."

They rushed up the street, their library books pressed into the crooks of their arms.

They slowed to a walk when they saw a German shepherd. They were scared of dogs. The German shepherd was carrying an orange tennis ball in its mouth.

Miata looked around. "Do you see his owner?" she asked.

"No," Ana answered. "He looks nice, doesn't he?" Ana relaxed because this dog looked friendly. He had started to wag his tail.

The dog went the other way, the orange ball still in its mouth. The girls watched the dog disappear and then started walking fast again.

They arrived at the school parking lot. It was surrounded by a tall chain-link fence. Miata and Ana put down their books and clung to the fence, looking in. Three large buses stood huge as billboards.

Miata and Ana looked around. The street was quiet except for a breeze in the sycamore trees. They rattled the locked gate.

"We can squeeze through," Miata said.

"Someone is going to see us," Ana said. She looked around, biting a fingernail. She saw a boy playing catch by himself on a front lawn.

Just then a car passed on the street. Ana wanted to run away. But Miata grabbed her wrist.

"Don't panic. Just do what I do," Miata whispered. The two of them pretended to be tying their shoes.

"Come on," Miata said when the car disappeared. "It'll just take a second."

"You go first," Ana said.

"Okay," Miata said. She groaned as she squeezed her body through the opening. First her head went in, then her foot, her shoulders, and, finally, her other foot.

Since Ana was smaller she slipped through the gate easily. But she had to slip back out. They had left their library books outside the gate.

"That's all we need," Ana said, passing the books to Miata. "We'd be in trouble for sure if we lost them."

They were now inside the gate. In one of the buses, they hoped, was the skirt that could save Miata from a scolding.

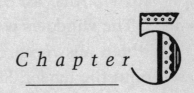

Chapter 5

The three yellow buses were too tall. Miata and Ana leaped up and down like frogs, but they couldn't see inside.

"I can't see a thing," Miata said.

Ana wrote her name in the grime that clung to the side of the bus. ANA MADRIGAL. Then she erased it with her hand. She knew that her name shouldn't be there.

"What are we going to do?" Ana asked Miata as they walked around the first bus. Ana stopped to kick the tire, and hurt her big toe.

"Easy," Miata said. "I'll look in from the window."

"How?" Ana asked. She craned her neck. The windows were too high.

Without answering, Miata boosted herself onto the fender. She started climbing onto the hood of the bus. The climb was as slippery as going up a slide the wrong way. The hood buckled and popped. The noise seemed deafening.

"You're making too much noise," Ana hissed. She looked around. She saw a car passing slowly on the street. Its radio was too loud for the driver to hear them.

Miata knew she was making a lot of noise. She didn't know what to do except to climb faster. Once on top, she cupped

her hands around her eyes. She peered through the dusty and insect-flecked windshield. She saw a math book, a crushed lunch bag, gum wrappers, and a pencil in the aisle.

"Do you see it?" Ana asked in a whisper.

"No," Miata answered flatly. She had scanned the inside of the bus, but saw nothing that looked like a skirt. She slid down the hood, nearly face first, to the ground. She brushed the gravel off her hands and ordered, "Let's check the next one."

Again Miata climbed onto a bus and gazed in. This time she saw a sweater, a baseball cap, and a smashed milk carton in the aisle. For a moment her heart fluttered because she thought she saw her skirt. But it was only a jacket on the floor.

"Do you see it?" Ana asked as she

looked around nervously. Two more cars passed. A diesel truck was rumbling up the street. Black smoke rose from its shiny chrome exhaust pipes.

The truck driver waved at Miata. Not knowing what to do, she waved back. "The driver saw us," she told Ana. She grew nervous and started climbing down.

"He saw you?" Ana asked in a loud voice. She turned around and saw the diesel truck rumbling away. Its taillights were dusty red. "Do you think he's going to call the police?"

"Nah," Miata answered. "Give me some room."

Miata slid down the hood. This time she fell on the gravel and skinned her knee.

"Ay!" she screamed. Blood the color of pomegranate juice began to rise to the surface of her skin. She hobbled on one leg, her face pinched from pain. Miata stopped and took a long breath. She pressed a thumb to the scrape and counted to ten.

"Are you all right?" Ana asked. She examined the scrape. A worry line rippled her brow.

"I'm okay," Miata answered, and counted in a whisper, ". . . *ocho* . . . *nueve* . . . *diez*." The blood had stopped flowing. She rose to her feet and said, "It's gotta be in that last bus."

Ana marched alongside a hobbling Miata. They were going to search the third bus.

"Let me look," Ana demanded.

Miata was surprised. She knew that Ana was scared of heights. Scared of the dark. Scared of dogs, cats, and thunder. Ana was scared of everything, it seemed to Miata.

Ana boosted herself onto the fender. She strained and grunted. The muscles in her skinny arms shivered. Her knees got dirty and hurt from pressing into the metal.

"You're almost there," Miata encouraged. "Keep going."

Ana climbed onto the hood and looked in through the windshield. She saw a book, a paper cup, and gum wrappers on the floor. Then she screamed, "It's there! In the back."

"You see it?" Miata yelled.

"Yeah!" Ana hollered.

In her excitement Ana lost her balance and rolled off the hood. Luckily she landed on her feet, just like a cat.

"That was cool," Miata said. "How did you do that?"

"I don't know," a dizzy Ana said. "How are we going to get in?"

"Easy," Miata answered. "You're going to squeeze your arm through the door and pull the lever that opens it."

"Me?" Ana asked, her eyes big.

"Your arms are smaller. You can do it."

Ana shrugged her shoulders and walked over to the door. She pushed her arm through the rubber gasket. Her fingers reached and reached for the lever.

"You can do it," Miata encouraged again.

Ana reached until her arm hurt from stretching. When her hand clasped the lever, she pulled and yanked. And Miata pulled and yanked on Ana.

The lever gave, and the door opened with a sigh.

"¡*Qué bueno*!" Miata cheered, hugging her friend. They smiled widely at each other.

Ana looked at the black marks on her arm. She rubbed the black off and said, "I'm going to take a bubble bath tonight."

Miata marched inside and snatched her

skirt off a seat. She pressed it to her waist and twirled, so that the skirt fanned out. She said to herself, "It's so pretty."

As she started to leave, Miata heard the sound of a car. Her heart leaped like a fish. Did someone see them? she wondered. Through the windows of the bus she saw her father's truck. He was with a man in a checkered shirt who was unlocking the gate.

"*¿Qué pasó?*" she said to Ana as she hurried off the bus.

Chapter 6

Miata's father revved the truck's engine, shifted into first gear, and slowly entered the unlocked gate. Bluish smoke coughed from the tailpipe.

The man in the checkered shirt locked the gate behind him. "That one over there," he bellowed. He pointed to the bus where Miata and Ana cowered.

Miata gripped her skirt and library books. Ana gripped Miata's hand in prayer. They tiptoed to the front of the bus, where they were out of sight.

The truck sounded like a tank as it moved toward the bus. Miata's father turned off its engine. The door opened with a squeak and then slammed closed. Heavy footsteps crunched against the gravel.

"What are they doing here?" Ana asked, biting a knuckle.

"I don't know," Miata answered. "Let me see." She peeked from behind the fender. Her father was putting on his heavy work gloves. The other man was tapping a flashlight against his thigh.

"Do you think we should surrender?" Ana asked. "They're going to find us."

Miata shook her head and pulled on Ana. They hurried to the far end of the

parking lot and hid behind a row of big oil drums. They watched the men unload welding equipment from the truck. Miata's father looked under the bus.

The man in the checkered shirt said, "Looks like someone was monkeying around here." He looked about the yard and kicked the loose gravel. A pebble ticked against one of the oil drums.

"He knows we're here," Ana whispered. Her small shoulders twitched like wings.

"They can't see us," Miata whispered back.

Miata's father popped the welder. A blue flame shot out. He adjusted the flame, lowered his goggles, and crawled under the bus. The bus was old and squeaky when it bounced on the road, and the frame was cracked from the weight of kids and time. A few sparks kicked against the ground.

"I'm scared of that noise," Ana whined. She pressed her hands to her ears. A single tear crawled down her cheek.

"Don't cry," Miata said. She held hands with Ana, who wiped away the tear.

Miata thought about that morning's breakfast. She remembered how her father had talked about a small job. Her father was always doing small jobs. He would weld broken bicycles, tractors, trailers, and farm equipment. He welded on Saturday, his day off.

"We'll wait until Dad's finished," Miata told Ana. "It won't be long."

They spread the skirt on the ground. The two of them sat on it, hugging their knees. The two friends had a history of experiencing similar trouble. They had both locked themselves out of their houses. They had both climbed trees and couldn't get down. They had both played with matches and burned their fingers. And they hadn't told anyone but each other.

But hiding from grown-ups in a parking lot was something new. They were both ready to cry, when they heard a slurping sound behind them.

They looked up through moist eyes. At the fence was Rodolfo. He was sipping a Coke through a straw. His hair was combed, his cheeks red as cinnamon red hots. He was on his bike and clinging to the fence.

"What are you guys doing?" he asked calmly. His slurping was nearly as loud as the welding. He let out a polite burp.

Miata and Ana were shocked to see him. "We're hiding," Miata whispered. "Be quiet."

"How come?" he asked. "You guys playing a game? Can I play?"

"No, we're not playing a game," Miata whispered angrily.

"We're in trouble because of you!" Ana snapped. "If you had left Miata alone, she wouldn't have forgotten her skirt on the bus."

"That's why you're hiding?" he asked. Rodolfo thought for a moment, then he suggested, "Why don't you crawl out here?" He pointed to a hole in the fence partially hidden by yellowish weeds.

Miata and Ana looked at each other. Their eyes were big with hope. They got to their feet.

Miata peeked over at her father and the man in the checkered shirt, who was unloading a heavy toolbox from the truck.

"You first," Miata said, turning to Ana. "I'll take your library books, and you take the skirt."

"I'm scared," Ana said.

"Don't be," Rodolfo said. "I'll give you some of my soda if you do it."

"I don't want any of your soda," Ana said. She sneered at Rodolfo. "I have plenty at home."

Ana breathed in deeply three times. Then she dashed for the hole, leaping over a stack of lumber. Miata followed closely, library books tucked under her arm like a football.

They heard someone shout, "Hey." It was the man in the checkered shirt. He dropped the toolbox and scattered the tools. The man cursed under his breath. He had dropped a heavy wrench on his big toe.

"Stop, you kids," he hollered.

But Miata and Ana didn't stop. They scrambled through the hole and didn't look back. They raced up the street alongside the shadow of Rodolfo's bike.

Chapter 7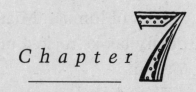

Miata and Ana ran to the library, where they tossed themselves on the lawn.

"That was close," Miata said after she caught her breath. Her cheeks were red, and her hair had come loose.

"Yes, that *was* close," Ana breathed. She was exhausted but relieved to get away.

They lay on their backs and stared at the blue sky, where high in the distance an airplane was a black speck against a white puff of cloud. They felt their heartbeats slow to a gallop and their breathing return to normal.

Rodolfo did figure eights while they rested. He was showing off by riding with his eyes closed. He hit the curb and sailed over the handlebars with his arms stretched out. He looked like Superman. But unlike Superman, he crashed with an "Ouch."

Miata and Ana sat up and asked, "Are you all right?"

"It didn't hurt," he said as he got up and dusted off his pants. A bump began to rise immediately on his forehead.

"Are you sure?" Miata asked.

"Yeah," he said. He walked his bicycle over and sat on the grass with them. The bump was pink and shiny and hot when Miata touched it. Ana made a face. She touched the bump too, but pulled her fingers away quickly.

"Isn't that your mom?" Rodolfo asked.

Miata and Ana followed Rodolfo's gaze. The woman leaving the library with an armful of books *was* Miata's mother. She was walking with a friend.

The three kids were sitting on the lawn in plain view. There was no escape.

"Hide," Miata whispered.

"Hide?" Ana asked.

"Just pretend you're asleep," Miata said. She lay down, opened a book, and placed it over her face. Miata was staring at a mouse. One of the books she had borrowed was about a mouse that had moved from a wheat farm to New York City.

Ana and Rodolfo did the same. Ana lay

still, but Rodolfo was giggling behind his book. His body shuddered from laughter.

Ana shivered like a leaf. She was scared of getting caught.

They heard footsteps on the sidewalk and then the voices of adults. Miata's mother and her friend were talking about the Sunday dance.

"I don't know what I'm going to do," Miata's mother said. "Miata plays so hard, and her legs are always full of scratches."

"Kids are so hard on their clothes," her mother's friend said. "I had to buy my daughter two pairs of shoes, and . . ."

Miata thought about the new scrape on her knee. It was true. She was always falling off the monkey bars or tripping over the garden hose, sliding into second base and coming up hurt, or climbing a fence and coming down face first. And it was true that the asphalt tore up her shoes.

Her new shoes were only a month old, but they already looked like her old shoes.

They heard a car door open. A few seconds later the engine started up with a roar. When the car backed out of its parking space, the three kids looked up.

Rodolfo sat up, with grass in his hair. He was reading the book that had covered his face. "This is pretty good," he said of the story about children lost at sea.

Miata and Ana got up, brushing grass off their skirts.

"Thanks, Rudy." Miata beamed. She started to walk away with Ana. Then she stopped and said, "I didn't know you were good at math."

"I'm better at shooting hoops," he said, getting onto his bike. "Let's play sometime."

Miata returned home with Ana.

"I'm going to throw the skirt on the

clothesline," Miata said. "It smells like the bus."

She pinned the skirt to the line. It whipped bright as a flag in the May wind.

Miata and Ana went inside. They were careful to wipe their feet. It was Saturday, the day her mother mopped the kitchen.

"Hi, honey," her mother greeted. She was at the kitchen table, opening the day's mail. "Hi, Ana. Are you ready for tomorrow?"

Miata and Ana looked at each other.

"I guess so," Ana said shyly.

Miata's mother took down two glasses from the cupboard. She got a plastic pitcher of lemonade from the refrigerator. She looked down at Miata's legs. "You scratched up your knee again?"

Miata looked down at her knees and said, "A little bit." She touched the scab

gently. She winced even though it didn't hurt.

"How did you do that?"

The secret almost spilled out. Instead, Miata spilled lemonade from the pitcher. Two ice cubes skated across the floor. The girls cleaned up the mess and went to the living room to read their library books.

Ana left when Little Joe came into the house. His knees were caked with mud. She knew that he was going to be in trouble for dragging in dirt.

"Ay, you little *chango*!" his mother cried. She made him undress on the back porch. He had to run from the porch to the bathtub in his underwear.

When Miata's father came home, he was whistling. He was happy because he had repaired a bus and earned a little extra money. He could look forward to a hundred-dollar check in next week's mail.

"It was easy," he said after a long swallow of water. He refilled his glass and continued. "It was just *zip*, and that baby was fixed in a minute. All because I'm the best welder in town."

Miata's mother smiled and said it was true. He was the best welder in the whole San Joaquin Valley. Little Joe came into the kitchen, a towel draped over his shoulders like a king's cape. He looked around and ran away. He had spotted a small shoeprint on the floor. And it looked like one of his.

"What a little monkey," his father said with affection. He turned to Miata, who was coloring at the kitchen table. "What did you do today?" he asked. "I saw you at the library with Ana. You two are going to dance like flowers tomorrow."

Miata stuttered, "Ah, well, I checked some books out. We just hung around. We didn't do anything."

"I'm glad I got a good daughter," her father said. "Some kids were fooling around on the buses."

Miata stopped coloring.

"Did you catch them?" her mother asked.

"Nah. Henry saw them, but I was busy welding."

Miata started coloring again. She was working on a picture of a tropical rain forest.

Her father sat down at the kitchen table. He said, "There were two girls and a boy on a bike."

Miata stopped coloring again.

"But you know how kids are," her father said. "They were just fooling around."

Miata started coloring again. Her mother said, "You know, I saw two girls and a boy at the library. I wonder if it was them?"

Miata stopped coloring again. This time she gathered her crayons and picture and left the kitchen. She couldn't stand to hear any more.

That night they had hamburgers, thick french fries, and root beer to wash it all down. After dinner her father turned on the television. Luckily for him and the rest of the Dodgers fans, it didn't rain in San Diego. Her father cuddled up on the couch with Little Joe and Miata. Although the Dodgers lost 4–3, it was something to do on a Saturday night.

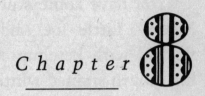

Chapter 8

Sunday morning. The family sat down early to *chorizo con huevos*. They ate happily in silence, pinching up their breakfast with ripped pieces of tortilla. The radio in the kitchen was softly playing Mexican songs.

Miata's mother took a sip of her coffee.

Then, getting up, she said, "Miata, I have a surprise for you."

Miata looked up. She had a little stain of ketchup in the corner of her mouth. Her mother went to the hall closet and returned with a crinkled bag.

"You have some stuff on your mouth, Miata," Little Joe said. His cheek was flecked with ketchup and the corners of his mouth stained white with milk.

Miata pressed a napkin to her mouth and ignored her brother. She was curious about the bag in her mother's hand.

"Now close your eyes," her mother said. Her smile was bright.

Miata closed her eyes. Maybe it was a new jacket, she thought. Maybe it was a Nintendo. Maybe it was a pair of new shoes. Her mother had been promising her new shoes.

When her mother patted her hand, she

opened her eyes. Her mother was holding up a skirt. A beautiful new *folklórico* skirt. The shiny lace rippled in the light. It smelled new. It was still stiff from not being worn.

"It's pretty, *mi'ja*," her father remarked. "You'll be the prettiest girl at the dance."

Miata forced a smile. "But I have a skirt, Mom."

"That old thing?" her mother said. "Stand up."

Her mother pressed the skirt to her waist. "It's a little long, but you can wear it just for today."

"It looks neat," Little Joe said. He now had ketchup on his elbows.

"Thanks, Mom," Miata said. She hugged her mother and went to her bedroom.

As Miata dressed for church she thought of all the trouble she went through to rescue her old skirt: slipping through the locked gate, rolling off the hood of the bus, getting scraped up. She remembered how they hid behind the oil barrel, and how Rodolfo just slurped on his soda while they were so scared. *Qué* bother! What a waste of time.

But it *is* pretty, she thought. She admired the new skirt that was fanned out on the bed. She liked the bright new colors and its fresh smell. She liked the rustle that sounded like walking through knee-high weeds. She pictured herself twirling in the middle of her friends.

She felt sorry for her old skirt. It was like a flower dead on its stem. She folded it carefully and put it in her bottom drawer. She brushed her hair and then stopped. She felt sad for her old skirt. It had belonged to her mother when she was a little girl.

She took it out of the bottom drawer. Next to the new skirt it looked faded as an old calendar. A blue stain darkened the hem. A piece of red lace was loose and falling off. The button was cracked. The skirt was smudged from time and wear.

"I'm going to take you both," she said. "I won't play favorites."

She pushed both of the skirts into her backpack. She finished combing her hair and put on her *milagro* earrings.

"*Ándale,*" her mother called from the living room. "We're going to be late."

Miata picked up her backpack and gave it a soft pat. "We're going dancing," she said to the skirts.

Miata's father was outside warming up their car. Little Joe was stomping on an empty soda can. He was trying to hook it onto the bottom of his shoe. His father called Little Joe to get in the car. Miata and her mother came hurrying down the steps. A bloom of perfume and beauty trailed behind them.

Miata went to church with her family. The priest talked and talked, but Miata yawned only three times. Tears of sleepiness came to her eyes. Her mother seemed happy. She kept looking down at Miata and Little Joe.

After church the dancers raced to the rectory, where they changed and practiced.

"Do your best," Mrs. Carranza, the dance teacher, said. "And remember to smile."

"Here we go," Miata said to Ana.

The six girls marched out to the courtyard. Their faces were bright. Their hair was coiled into buns. They stood in a circle with their hands on their hips. As the cassette music played, Miata spun around

the courtyard. The grown-ups and kids all ate donuts and watched.

Miata twirled like a pinwheel, the old skirt showing under the new skirt. Miata was wearing both of them. Her mother recognized the old skirt and clapped and smiled proudly at her daughter. And everyone, even the babies, clapped for the spinning colors of Mexico.